Text copyright © 2015 by Harriet Ziefert
Illustrations copyright © 2015 by Christina O Donovan
All rights reserved / CIP date is available.
Published in the United States by
🍎 Blue Apple Books
515 Valley Street, Maplewood, NJ 07040
www.blueapplebooks.com

First Edition
Printed in China 02/15
Hardcover ISBN: 978-1-60905-512-7
Paperback ISBN: 978-1-60905-579-0
1 3 5 7 9 10 8 6 4 2

Are You My Brown Bear?

¿Eres Mi Oso Pardo?

by **Harriet Ziefert**

illustrations by
Christina O Donovan

BLUE 🍎 APPLE

Are you my brown bear?

¿Eres tú mi oso pardo?

No! I am black bear.

¡No! Soy oso negro.

And I am white bear.

Y yo soy oso blanco.

I am not brown bear!

¡No soy oso pardo!

Are you my brown bear?

¿Eres tú mi oso pardo?

No! I am fuzzy bear.

¡No! Soy oso crespo.

I am buzzy bear.

Soy oso zumbador.

I am hairy bear.

Soy oso peludo.

I am scary bear.

Soy oso espeluznante.

I am baby bear.
Soy oso bebé.

I am not brown bear!

¡No soy oso pardo!

I am on-my-way bear.

Soy oso en-mi-camino.

I am gray bear.

Soy oso gris.

Are you my brown bear?
¿Eres tu mi oso pardo?

No. I am wet bear.
No. Soy oso mojado.

I am pet bear.
Soy oso mascota.

I am boy bear.

Yo soy oso niño.

I am toy bear.

Soy oso de juguete.

Look at me!
My fur is brown.

¡Mírame!
Mi pelo es de color marrón.

I am your brown bear!

¡Yo soy tu oso pardo!

I am your teddy bear!
¡Yo soy tu osito de peluche!